Snow White's New Friend

By Lara Bergen
Illustrated by the Disney Storybook Artists

Random House 🏠 New York

Copyright © 2010 Disney Enterprises, Inc. All rights reserved. Published in the United States by Random House Children's Books, a division of Random House, Inc., 1745 Broadway, New York, NY 10019,and in Canada by Random House of Canada Limited, Toronto, in conjunction with Disney Enterprises, Inc. Random House and the colophon are registered trademarks of Random House, Inc.
Library of Congress Control Number: 2009927207
ISBN: 978-0-7364-2654-1
www.randomhouse.com/kids
MANUFACTURED IN CHINA
10 9 8 7 6 5 4 3 2 1

Ariel's Dolphin Adventure

By Lyra Spenser
Illustrated by the Disney Storybook Artists

Random House 🏠 New York

Copyright © 2010 Disney Enterprises, Inc. All rights reserved. Published in the United States by Random House Children's Books, a division of Random House, Inc., 1745 Broadway, New York, NY 10019, and in Canada by Random House of Canada Limited, Toronto, in conjunction with Disney Enterprises, Inc. Random House and the colophon are registered trademarks of Random House, Inc.
Library of Congress Control Number: 2009927207
ISBN: 978-0-7364-2654-1
www.randomhouse.com/kids
MANUFACTURED IN CHINA
10 9 8 7 6 5 4 3 2 1

"Oh, Eric! This is wonderful!" Ariel exclaimed as she twirled around the ballroom with her prince. "I can dance with you and see the ocean at the same time!"

Eric knew that although Ariel was happy on land, she missed her sea friends. He wished there was some way his princess could have the best of both worlds. . . .

A few weeks later, Eric had a surprise for Ariel.
He took her to the lagoon, which was now protected
by a big wall he had built around it. The wall kept
dangerous sharks out. But a small gate allowed
little sea creatures, such as Ariel's friends,
to safely swim up and visit with the princess.
In fact, Flounder and Sebastian were already
there to greet her, along with Scuttle!

Ariel was so excited to see her friends
that she jumped right into the water.
Then she noticed a baby dolphin. He was
all alone and seemed scared.

"His mother probably can't fit through
the gate," Ariel said. "She must be on the
other side of the wall."

"Don't worry, Ariel," said Flounder.
"We'll find the dolphin's mother!"

Days passed, and Sebastian and Flounder still hadn't found the baby dolphin's mother. Ariel watched, heartbroken, as the little dolphin swam sadly around the lagoon.

That night, a fierce storm came. Ariel and Eric rushed to the lagoon, where they found Flounder trying to calm the scared baby dolphin. Eric felt terrible. He realized he had made a mistake by building a wall around the lagoon.

"I need to ask my father for help," Ariel told the prince. "Please watch over the baby dolphin while I'm gone."

Ariel carefully climbed onto the wall of the lagoon and called out to the ocean. "Help me, please! I am Ariel, Princess of the Seas. I need my father, King Triton. Please help!"

Immediately, sea creatures big and small swam through the rough waters to find King Triton.

Back at the lagoon, Eric was doing his best to keep the baby dolphin safe from the crashing waves.

Suddenly, there was a flash of light, and the storm cleared.

King Triton had arrived!

"What has happened here?" King Triton roared.

Eric looked down humbly. "It is my fault, sir," he explained. "I built this wall to make a safe place for Ariel's friends. I never meant for this to happen."

The King of the Seas glared at Eric. Then, with a hint of a smile, he said, "Well, you are human, after all."

King Triton called to all the dolphins, who quickly found the baby's mother. She had tried frantically to get into the lagoon but, as Ariel had guessed, was too large to fit through the gate. "Swim back, everyone!" shouted the king. He raised his trident and blasted the wall to pieces.

There was no royal ball at the palace that night. Instead, Eric and
Ariel stayed by the lagoon and danced under the sparkling stars.
Sebastian and his orchestra provided the music, King Triton clapped,
and the baby dolphin—safe beside his mother—gave the prince and
princess a playful splash.

"I think that means we are forgiven!" Ariel said with a laugh.

". . . and then having them return for
lots and lots of visits!"

Snow White tried her best to comfort Dopey. "Don't worry," she
told him. "Remember, I went away, too. But I still come back and visit.
Being a good friend sometimes means letting your friends go . . ."

Dopey smiled and held out his hand. But instead of climbing onto his finger, as it had done when it was a caterpillar, the butterfly flew away.

Suddenly, a tiny creature began to push its way out of the shell.

Slowly but surely, its small, damp wings began to open up. They grew larger and larger. Then, very gently, they flapped forward and back. Dopey's furry friend was now a beautiful butterfly!

"Oh, how wonderful!" said Snow White. "When a caterpillar goes
into its shell, that means it's ready to turn into a butterfly!"
Dopey and the other Dwarfs couldn't believe their ears!

Dopey took Snow White's hand and led her out of the cottage to a tree. He pointed to a branch, where a hard, shiny shell was hanging.

True to her word, one month later, Snow White and the Prince visited the Seven Dwarfs at their cottage. As the princess handed out heart-shaped cookies, she noticed that Dopey looked sad—and that something was missing.

"Dopey, where is our little caterpillar friend?" Snow White asked.

Everyone ate and danced and played
music and had a lovely afternoon. Dopey
even made sure the caterpillar had a
delicious leaf to nibble on. When it was time
for the Dwarfs to go home, Snow White
gave each one a kiss. "I promise to visit you
soon," she told them.

"Dopey! We were so worried!"
Snow White exclaimed. Then
she noticed a fuzzy caterpillar
crawling across a leaf and onto
Dopey's finger.

Dopey had found a new
friend to bring to the picnic.

Snow White and the six Dwarfs
searched everywhere for Dopey.
Finally, Grumpy found him in a
corner of the palace garden.

"Here he is!" hollered Grumpy.
"I'm starvin'. Let's eat."

Snow White led the Dwarfs to the picnic and began to hand out plates. "One for Doc . . . and Happy . . . and Sleepy . . . and Bashful . . . and Grumpy . . . and Sneezy . . . and— Oh, my! Where is Dopey?"

One bright spring day, Snow White and her prince invited the Seven Dwarfs to the palace for a picnic. Snow White had not seen the Dwarfs in quite some time, and she had missed her friends.

"Thank you for inviting us, Your Highness!" said Doc.

"I'm so glad you came," Snow White replied with a smile. "I can't wait to show you the wonderful food we have out on the lawn!"